Schoolyard Science

Schoolyard Science

Peggy K. Perdue

Illustrations by
Karen Waiksnis DiSorbo
Foreword by
Diane A. Vaszily

Scott, Foresman and Company
Glenview, Illinois London

A GOOD YEAR BOOK®

Good Year Books
are available for preschool through grade 12 and for every basic curriculum subject plus many enrichment areas. For more Good Year Books, contact your local bookseller or educational dealer. For a complete catalog with information about other Good Year Books, please write:

Good Year Books
Scott, Foresman and Company
1900 East Lake Avenue
Glenview, Illinois 60025

To Broward County Soil and Water Conservation District

---

1 2 3 4 5 6 EBI 95 94 93 92 91 90

ISBN 0-673-38967-7

Contents

Foreword

Schoolyard Science invites you and your students to experience the environment right outside the school building. Although we're surrounded by nature, we often tend to overlook its wonders through either indifference or overfamiliarity. The activities in this book (designed to be used by elementary school teachers in outdoor settings of all types) will awaken an awareness of nature's wonders. The most important ingredient in sparking student enthusiasm, however, will always be you—the teacher.

While outdoor science experiences must always have a specific focus, try not to overteach or overdirect students. Allow them to discover nature on their own by weaving these activities into the discovery process. In addition, be careful not to overemphasize identification by proper scientific names. Encourage students to use names like "Blaine" or "Gabrielle" for unknown trees and plants. Have them pay more attention to the characteristics that make the specimen unique. And here's a hint for making these activities even more exciting. Invite your students to "dress" for the event! Encourage the wearing of safari-like outfits—complete with hats, binoculars, notepads, collecting bags, and even cameras—to add an element of adventure to their outdoor experience.

Each activity in **Schoolyard Science** is structured to help children develop social, thinking, and process skills. You can encourage the development of cooperative social skills by placing students in teams of three or four. Refer to team members as "colleagues," and encourage "collaboration" when they venture out on an expedition. Relate what they are doing to the actual work of scientific teams in the field. To be effective, each team should collect the data for the activity; then, if necessary, the various teams can compile, compare, and average their findings. Be sure to emphasize how crucial the charting, graphing, and analysis of data are to effective use of the scientific method.

To promote thinking and process skills, avoid giving specific directions for the activity. Instead, simply state the objective as you hand out the Student Lab Sheet. Make sure each team has a general idea of how to collect the data; then encourage creative collaboration. If a team appears to need assistance, offer a few open-ended suggestions—but always allow team members to make the decisions. Remember, it is only when students do the work themselves that they truly gain understanding.

Consider planning just one or two activities for your first outdoor expedition. This first venture should aim primarily at familiarizing students with your procedures and what you expect of them. It is your role to serve as their guide to learning, helping them to enjoy the wonders of nature and getting them to realize that those wonders are everywhere—even on their own schoolyard! Once they have experienced science on the schoolyard, students will look at their environment (and, hopefully, the world) in a different, more caring, and more concerned way.

Diane A. Vaszily
The Science Eye

How to Use This Book

Schoolyard Science is just what you need to turn the great outdoors into your science classroom. Lab activities include working with the weather, soil, plants, animals, and the environment. Since each lab stands on its own, you can use the activities in any sequence; you may even allow students to decide which labs they would like to do and in what order.

The activities in **Schoolyard Science** may be done by individuals or by lab teams of three or four students. Although designed for students in grades two through four, these labs have worked quite successfully with students in all the elementary grades in schools in all types of environments.

Each activity consists of two basic components: teacher information and a corresponding Student Lab Sheet. The teacher information (purposely concise so that you can set up and implement labs without a great deal of reading) is divided into sections. A brief introduction provides an overview of the lab's major concept. Needed supplies are listed under the heading "Materials." If you want students to work individually, you may decide to set out the materials at the learning center ready for use. If you want students to work in lab teams (or if space is limited), you can label and store the materials; the team can then designate one member to gather all the supplies for the activity. This same student would then be responsible for making sure that all materials are returned to their proper locations upon completion of the lab.

The next section of the teacher information comes under the heading "Preparation." This is where you'll learn what–if any–advance preparation you must perform. While you may find that your students are able to do most of the preparation themselves, you would be wise to give each lab a trial run before presenting it to your class. You may find that a slight modification would make the activity better suited to the specific students in your class.

"Answers to Student Lab Sheet"–the next section of the teacher information–gives possible answers to the questions posed on the Student Lab Sheet. Keep in mind that answers will vary and that vocabulary can differ greatly depending on the age of the student. Nevertheless, you may want to post this section to allow students to evaluate their own answers. A post-lab conference to evaluate comprehension may be used to supplement an evaluation based on these answers. The following section–headed "Super Scientist Activities"–provides possible answers for the extension activities on the Student Lab Sheet; these answers conclude the teacher information component of the activity.

The Student Lab Sheets, created in such a way as to nurture the scientific method of thinking, also begin with a brief introduction to the major focus of the activity. Then, under the "Materials" heading, students find a list of the items they will need for the lab. Encourage your students to inventory their supplies prior to starting the lab. They should ask themselves whether they have all the supplies and whether the supplies are set up as indicated on the lab sheet.

The next heading on the Student Lab Sheets is "Procedures." Here are the sequential steps that students must read and follow. At first, students may be unsure of themselves and seek constant reassurance from you. Emphasize, however, that following directions is an important skill they must learn for all their subjects, not just for science. Then direct them back to the Procedures. They may find the illustrations on the Student Lab Sheets of help in understanding the written instructions.

A large blank area bearing the heading "Record Your Observations" allows students to create a permanent record of what they observe during the lab. Observations take on a new meaning once they are recorded, and this area permits the recording of observations in a variety of ways. Students may place drawings, charts, graphs, or photographs in this space in addition to their own written commentary. Whatever form this record of observations takes, it will allow students to recall the activity and its results at a later date.

Although they may need your help initially, it is very important that students learn how to design their own charts and graphs as soon as possible. With this in mind, you may want to assign the recording method for students to use in order to ensure that students get practice in each method. Later on, however, you can relax this requirement and let each child decide which recording method is most appropriate for the activity.

Every Student Lab Sheet lists "Questions to Answer." The questions are designed to help focus observations while allowing the student to think independently about what he or she has just witnessed. Students should write their answers on the lab sheet in the space provided.

The last section of the Student Lab Sheets is entitled "Super Scientist Activities." These are extension activities that you can use to integrate the lab with other school subjects or to encourage creative problem solving. You can even use these activities as a basis for expanding the lab into a unit of study. You need not, of course, assign all the Super Scientist Activities. Pick and choose specific ones as you see fit or encourage students to select the ones that they find particularly intriguing.

Initially, you'd probably be well-advised to use the Student Lab Sheets in their original format. As your students gain confidence in the scientific method of problem solving, however, you may become a bit more daring. For example, try covering the step-by-step directions before duplicating the Student Lab Sheets, and then see if students can design their own procedures. This teaching technique will further stretch students' creative problem-solving skills.

Finally, while nothing can replace the experience of getting outside to study nature, you can enrich your science curriculum through judicious use of videos, filmstrips, movies, and supplementary books. Check with your school librarian regarding science reference books appropriate to students in the elementary grades. There are several good ones that can help students with plant and animal identification. Many of these books, moreover, are inexpensive enough for you to buy and keep in your classroom.

PHYSICAL SCIENCE

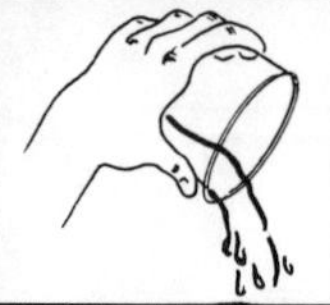

2

Only the Shadow Knows!

Most elementary school students have played shadow tag. This lab will lead to a deeper understanding of shadows as students observe and measure how a shadow changes throughout the day. At night shadows make imaginations come alive, but be sure to try this lab on a sunny day!

MATERIALS PER LAB TEAM

Yard or meter stick
Craft sticks or twigs (lots)

MATERIALS PER STUDENT

Student Lab Sheet 1.1
Pencil

PREPARATION

Duplicate Student Lab Sheet 1.1.

ANSWERS TO STUDENT LAB SHEET

1. The shadow changes in both size and location as the day progresses.
2. The shadow is at its longest and most narrow early in the morning and late in the afternoon. It is at its shortest and widest close to noon.

SUPER SCIENTIST ACTIVITIES

1. Graphs will be specific to your class. Check that students have completed the graph accurately and labeled both axes correctly.
2. Students can build a simple sundial using a straw and a drink lid from a fast-food restaurant. Using the lid as the base for the sundial, students stick the straw (cut in half) through the hole in the lid so that the portion above the lid casts a shadow. The students must then calibrate the sundial by comparing the shadow to the time on a regular clock. Encourage interested students to look up sundials in a reference book and create a more elaborate one on their own.

3

Rain, Rain, Go Away

How much rain falls during a rainstorm? The only way to find out is to measure. In this lab, students will make a simple rain gauge to record rainfall.

MATERIALS PER LAB TEAM

Clear plastic drinking glass (with straight sides)
Plastic ruler
Permanent marker

MATERIALS PER STUDENT

Student Lab Sheet 1.2
Pencil

PREPARATION

Students should be able to read a ruler. They should also know that when measuring a liquid, it is important to set the container on a level surface and to read the amount at eye level. Duplicate Student Lab Sheet 1.2.

ANSWERS TO STUDENT LAB SHEET

1. Buildings and trees can block the rain, producing an inaccurate measurement.
2. Answer will vary.
3. Answer will vary. In fact, answers may vary among classmates.

SUPER SCIENTIST ACTIVITIES

1. Graphs will be specific to your class. Check that students have completed the graph accurately and labeled both axes correctly.
2. No answer is necessary.
3. Answers will vary. Don't be surprised if home and school measurements are quite different.

4

Cool, Clear Water

Rain is nature's way of cleansing the Earth. Or is it? How clean is the rain that falls? Students will decide the answer as they collect and filter rain water.

MATERIALS PER LAB TEAM

Plastic drinking glasses, 2
Paper towel
Funnel
Magnifying glass

MATERIALS PER STUDENT

Student Lab Sheet 1.3
Pencil

PREPARATION

Cut the top 1/4 off a two-liter soda bottle for each team to use as a funnel. Duplicate Student Lab Sheet 1.3.

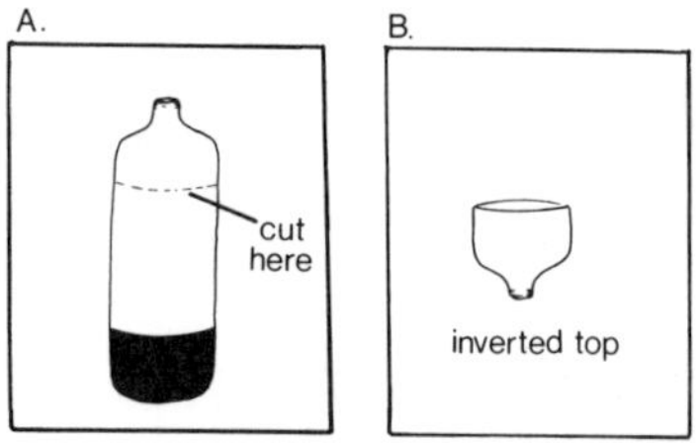

Students may need to be instructed on how to turn a paper towel into a paper filter. They should first fold the paper towel into fourths, forming a square. They next hold the corner with all the folds in one hand and cut a quarter circle from the bottom corner to the diagonal top corner. Still holding the corner, they pull the first layer of paper towards themselves. The "hole" that appears is where the water is to be poured.

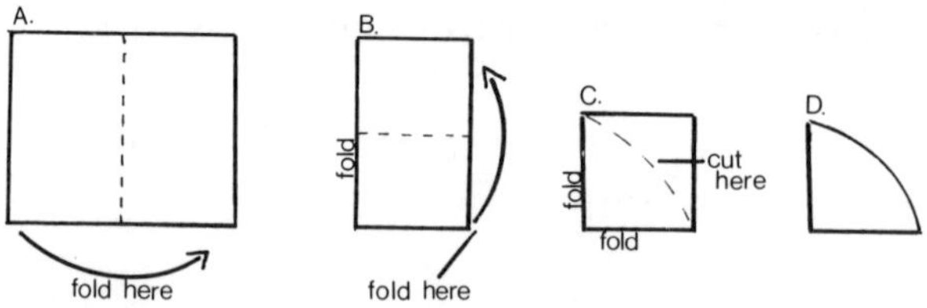

ANSWERS TO STUDENT LAB SHEET

1. In general, all water contains particles of foreign matter. Whether students are able to see any particles will depend on the enlargement capabilities of the magnifying glass they use.
2. Answers will vary.

SUPER SCIENTIST ACTIVITIES

1. Answers will vary. Look for clear charts that students have labeled correctly.
2. No answer is necessary. Check with your local waste water treatment plant for descriptive information.

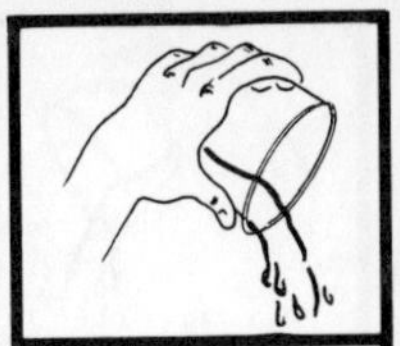

Do You Know Where You're Going?

This lab will give students hands-on experience in measuring, map reading, and map drawing as they design a map of the "outdoor classroom."

MATERIALS PER LAB TEAM

Tape measure

MATERIALS PER STUDENT

Student Lab Sheet 1.4
Pencil

PREPARATION

Bring in a variety of maps for students to examine. Point out the symbols that mapmakers use to represent actual objects. Students should be familiar with a map legend and its function. Duplicate Student Lab Sheet 1.4.

ANSWERS TO STUDENT LAB SHEET

1. Answers will vary depending on the students' creativity level.
2. To make the map as accurate as possible, students would need to take measurements and then draw the map to scale.

SUPER SCIENTIST ACTIVITIES

1. Check the legend of the map for accuracy.
2. The map should include the major landmarks on school property.
3. If students can find each other's treasure, their map drawing and map reading skills must be good.

6

Sunny Side Up

The Earth absorbs heat from the sun. In this lab, students will practice reading and recording the temperature of the ground throughout the day to determine if the amount of heat absorbed changes.

MATERIALS PER LAB TEAM

Thermometer

MATERIALS PER STUDENT

Student Lab Sheet 1.5
Pencil

PREPARATION

Students should be able to read a thermometer prior to the lab.
Duplicate Student Lab Sheet 1.5.

ANSWERS TO STUDENT LAB SHEET

1. No, the temperature varies.
2. Changes may occur for a number of reasons—e.g., cloudiness, shadows cast by other objects, and location of the sun.
3. Temperature changes alert animals to the time of day and the time of year.

SUPER SCIENTIST ACTIVITIES

1. Graphs will vary. Check that students have completed their graphs accurately and labeled both axes correctly. Also check to make sure that they drew line graphs as opposed to bar graphs.
2. The ground temperature decreases after the sun goes down.

7

You're Getting Warmer!

When a meteorologist reports that the local temperature is 78°, we often expect the temperature to be 78° where we are. But the temperature can vary within a given area. In this lab, students will predict the locations of the "hot spots" and "cold spots" of their outdoor classroom—and then measure to determine the accuracy of their predictions!

MATERIALS PER LAB TEAM

Thermometer
Craft sticks, 2
Blue construction paper
Red construction paper

MATERIALS PER STUDENT

Student Lab Sheet 1.6
Pencil

PREPARATION

Choose the shape for a flag, and have students use red construction paper to make "hot" flags and blue construction paper to make "cold" flags. Students should then label their flags and attach them to craft sticks. Duplicate Student Lab Sheet 1.6.

ANSWERS TO STUDENT LAB SHEET

1. Answers will vary, but most students will say they placed their flags based on how the air felt on their skin.
2. Answers will vary.
3. Several factors influence temperature, including sun location, number and frequency of clouds, and proximity to objects that create strong shadows.

SUPER SCIENTIST ACTIVITIES

1. Student maps should show the locations of their flags.
2. Answers will vary.
3. Although answers will vary, generally hot and cold spots change from month to month. As a result, this activity provides a great visual reminder of seasonal changes.

Student Lab Sheets

PHYSICAL SCIENCE

Name ______________________ Date ______________________ STUDENT LAB SHEET 1.1

Only the Shadow Knows!

Quick! Look over your shoulder! What's that shadow lurking in the corner? In this lab, you will study shadows and how they change. When you finish, perhaps the night won't seem quite so scary!

MATERIALS

Yard or meter stick
Craft sticks or twigs
Pencil

PROCEDURES

1. Start this lab in the morning of a sunny day.
2. Make an outline of a plant's shadow using craft sticks or twigs.
3. Measure the length and width of the shadow.
4. Repeat steps 2 and 3 every hour.

RECORD YOUR OBSERVATIONS

QUESTIONS TO ANSWER

1. Does the shadow stay the same or change?

2. When is the shadow the longest?

   Shortest?

   Widest?

   Narrowest?

SUPER SCIENTIST ACTIVITIES

1. Make a graph of your results.
2. Design and build a sundial. How accurate is it?

Name ______________________________ Date ______________________________

STUDENT LAB SHEET 1.2

Rain, Rain, Go Away

It's raining, it's pouring . . . but just how much? In this lab, you will become a meteorologist and measure the rainfall with a rain gauge that you've made!

MATERIALS

Clear plastic drinking glass (with straight sides)
Plastic ruler
Permanent marker
Pencil

PROCEDURES

1. Set the glass outside (away from any trees or buildings) on a day when rain seems likely.
2. Support the glass so that it will not tip over. Do this by building up the soil all around it.
3. After the rain stops, set the glass on a level surface.
4. Insert a plastic ruler inside the glass.
5. Measure the rainfall.

RECORD YOUR OBSERVATIONS

QUESTIONS TO ANSWER

1. Why should the glass be away from buildings and trees?

2. How much rain fell?

3. How does your measurement compare with the meteorologist's measurement?

SUPER SCIENTIST ACTIVITIES

1. Keep track of the amount of rainfall each month. Make a graph that shows your findings.
2. Visit a weather bureau to see the instruments that professional meteorologists use.
3. Keep track of rainfall at home. How do your home and school measurements compare?

Name ______________________ Date ______________________

STUDENT LAB SHEET 1.3

Cool, Clear Water

Rain is nature's way of cleansing the Earth. Or is it? How clean is the rain that falls? You decide the answer as you collect and filter rain water.

MATERIALS

Plastic drinking glasses, 2
Paper towel
Funnel
Magnifying glass
Pencil

PROCEDURES

1. Collect rainwater in one of the plastic glasses.
2. Fold and cut the paper towel to fit in the funnel. The towel will act as your filter paper.
3. Put the funnel over the other (empty) plastic glass.
4. Pour the rain water into the funnel.
5. Remove the paper towel from the funnel and allow it to dry.
6. Examine the paper towel with a magnifying glass.

RECORD YOUR OBSERVATIONS

QUESTIONS TO ANSWER

1. Are you able to see any particles trapped by the filter?

____

____

2. Can you identify any of the particles?

____

____

____

SUPER SCIENTIST ACTIVITIES

1. Test samples of water collected from the tap, a canal, a puddle, and the ocean. Compare the results.
2. Investigate how waste water is treated in your community.

Name ______________________________ Date ______________________

STUDENT LAB SHEET 1.4

Do You Know Where You're Going?

Can you read a map? Better yet, can you draw one? In this lab, you will make a map of the school property. And when you're finished, don't forget to put in the funny folds!

MATERIALS

Tape measure
Pencil

PROCEDURES

1. Measure the perimeter (outside edge) of the outdoor classroom.
2. Make a map of the area, using symbols to show the location of major landmarks.
3. Don't forget to include a legend to explain the meaning of your symbols!

RECORD YOUR OBSERVATIONS

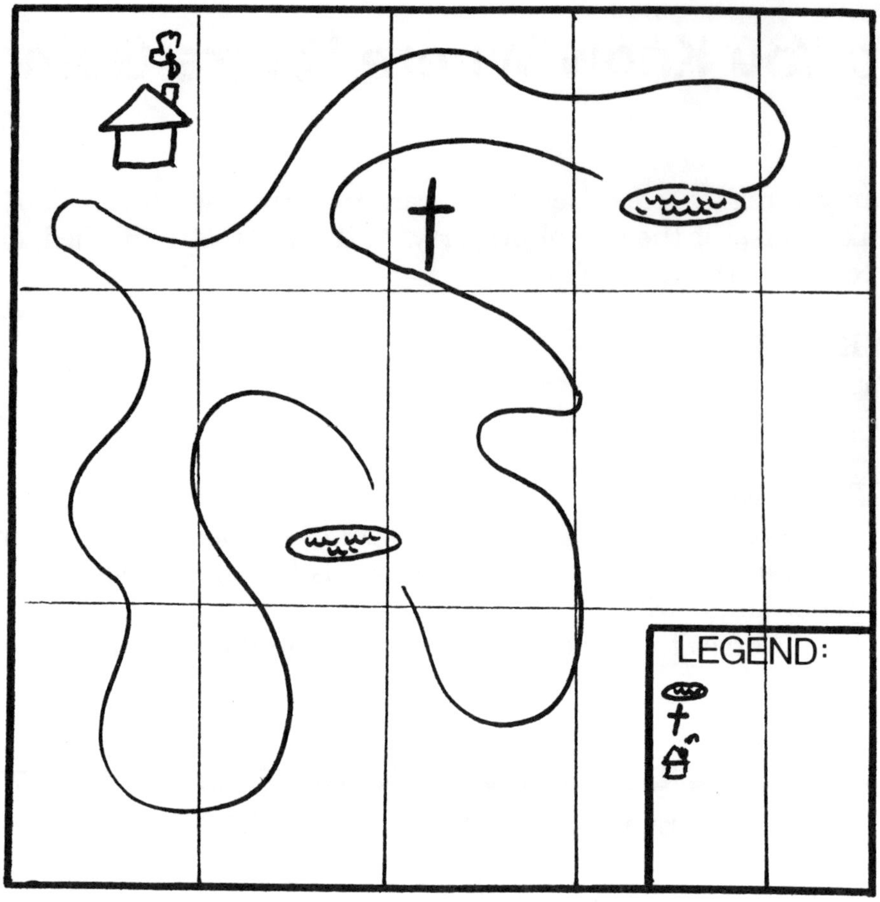

QUESTIONS TO ANSWER

1. What map symbols would be the best to use?

____

____

____

2. How can you make the map as accurate as possible?

____

____

____

SUPER SCIENTIST ACTIVITIES

1. Draw your map to scale.
2. Map the entire school grounds.
3. Have a "treasure hunt." Draw a map that shows the way to your treasure, and then exchange maps with someone else!

Name ______________________ Date ______________________ STUDENT LAB SHEET 1.5

Sunny Side Up

The Earth absorbs heat from the sun. Does that mean the ground temperature stays the same all day? With this lab you will go outside and find out!

MATERIALS

Thermometer
Pencil

PROCEDURES

1. Start this experiment early in the day.
2. Gently bury part of the thermometer in the ground so that soil covers the bulb.
3. Wait five minutes.
4. Read and record the temperature on the thermometer.
5. Return to the thermometer once each hour throughout the day to read and record the temperature.

RECORD YOUR OBSERVATIONS

QUESTIONS TO ANSWER

1. Does the temperature stay the same throughout the day?

____

____

2. If the temperature changes, what causes the change?

____

____

____

3. How would temperature changes in the ground affect plant and animal life?

____

____

____

____

SUPER SCIENTIST ACTIVITIES

1. Show the results of your temperature readings in a line graph.
2. Repeat the experiment at home. Continue to take temperature readings after the sun goes down. What happens to the ground temperature in the evening?

Name ______________________________ Date ______________________

You're Getting Warmer!

When a meteorologist reports that the temperature is 65°, does that mean it's 65° where you are? In this lab, you will predict the locations of the hot and cold spots on school property. Then you'll measure to find out whether your predictions were right.

MATERIALS

Thermometer
Craft sticks, 2
Blue construction paper
Red construction paper
Pencil

PROCEDURES

1. Place your "hot" flag at what you think is the warmest spot outside.
2. Place your "cold" flag at what you believe is the coolest spot.
3. Use a thermometer to measure the temperature in several locations around the school to check whether your predictions were right.

RECORD YOUR OBSERVATIONS

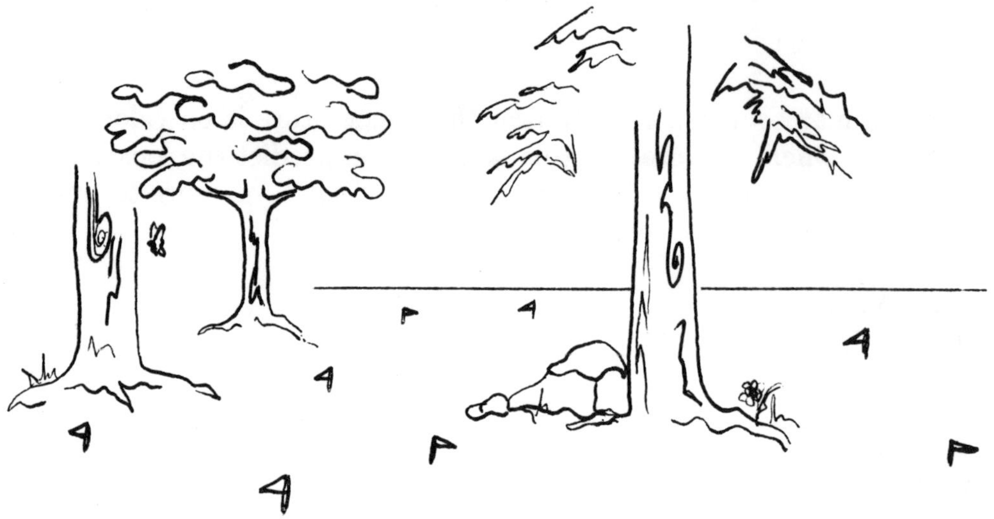

QUESTIONS TO ANSWER

1. What helped you figure out where to place your flags?

____

____

____

2. How close were your flags to the hottest and coolest locations?

____

____

3. What factors influence the temperature in a particular location?

____

____

____

SUPER SCIENTIST ACTIVITIES

1. Make a map of your findings.
2. Repeat the experiment at different times throughout the day. How do your results compare?
3. Repeat the experiment the first of each month. Are the hottest and coolest places always the same?

SOIL SCIENCE

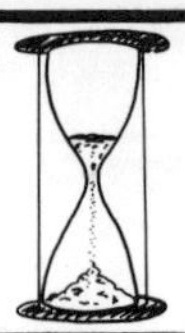

Running Interference

Animals (especially humans) affect the absorption rate of an area by compressing the soil. In this lab, students will time the water absorption rate in an area that animals use and compare their finding with the rate for an area that animals do not use.

MATERIALS PER LAB TEAM

Two soup cans (ends removed)
Centimeter ruler
Water
Plastic drinking glass
Empty 35mm film container
Watch with second hand

MATERIALS PER STUDENT

Student Lab Sheet 2.1
Pencil

PREPARATION

Collect soup cans. Remove both ends and any sharp edges from the cans. Duplicate Student Lab Sheet 2.1.

ANSWERS TO STUDENT LAB SHEET

1. There may be several differences. Students should have noticed that the ground where animals walked was more packed down. Plant life may have disappeared.
2. The area having less animal activity absorbed water more quickly.

SUPER SCIENTIST ACTIVITIES

1. Graphs will be specific to your class. Check that students have completed their graphs accurately and have labeled both axes correctly.
2. The answer will depend on the ground's saturation level.

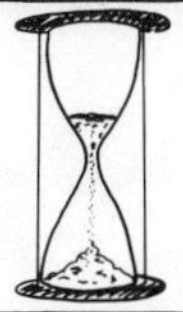

23

Hold It!

The ability of soil to retain water helps slow the erosion process. In this lab, students will collect soil samples from around the schoolyard and compare the amount of water in each.

MATERIALS PER LAB TEAM

Spade
Empty 35mm film container
Baby food jar with lid
Label

MATERIALS PER STUDENT

Student Lab Sheet 2.2
Pencil

PREPARATION

Collect empty baby food jars and 35mm film containers (a company that processes film often will save them for you on request). Clean the jars and remove their labels. At the conclusion of the experiment, encourage students to return the soil as close as possible to where they collected it. Duplicate Student Lab Sheet 2.2.

ANSWERS TO STUDENT LAB SHEET

1. Water was on the sides of the jar.
2. The water came from the soil.
3. Answers will vary depending on the soils used in the experiment.
4. The more water the soil absorbs, the less water will run off. Erosion occurs when water runs off, carrying soil with it.

SUPER SCIENTIST ACTIVITIES

1. Students should pour the water off, measure it, and record their findings.
2. Responses will vary.
3. In general, the smaller the soil particles, the more water the soil will retain. The reason is that more small soil particles can fit in a given area. The more particles, the more surface area for water to cling to.

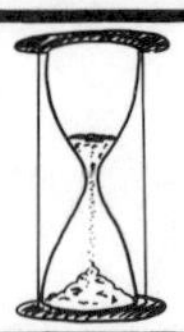

24

Drinking It All In

The more water soil absorbs, the less water will run off and carry soil with it. In this lab, students will conduct a test to determine which soil has the highest rate of water absorption.

MATERIALS PER LAB TEAM

Soup can with both ends removed
Water
Watch with second hand
Empty 35mm film container
Centimeter ruler
Permanent marker
Plastic drinking glass

MATERIALS PER STUDENT

Student Lab Sheet 2.3
Pencil

PREPARATION

Find several areas of open ground on school property to test. Ask students to bring in clean, empty soup cans with both ends removed. Have the students measure three centimeters up from the bottom edge of the can and draw a circle around the outside of the can at that point with the marker. Duplicate Student Lab Sheet 2.3.

ANSWERS TO STUDENT LAB SHEET

1. The can limits the amount of run-off that can occur.
2. By marking all the cans in the same place, students made sure that the set-up for the experiment would be the same for everyone. This is how scientists control variables.
3. Answers will vary.
4. Answers will vary.
5. The faster the soil absorbs water, the less water will run off and carry soil with it. In addition, soil that absorbs water quickly will also allow more air to reach plant roots.

SUPER SCIENTIST ACTIVITIES

1. Graphs will be specific to your class. Check that students have completed the graph accurately and labeled both axes correctly. Also make sure that the graphs are line graphs as opposed to bar graphs.
2. Answers will vary depending on the type of soil tested and the amount of rainfall prior to the experiment.
3. Answers will vary.

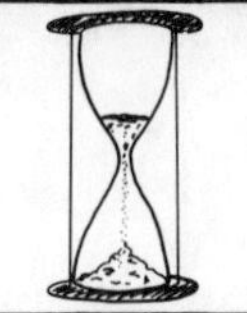

Just Weight!

Soil layering does not happen haphazardly. When soil particles are carried by wind and water, the heavier particles fall out first. In this lab, students will observe and measure how the particles layer themselves.

MATERIALS PER LAB TEAM

Plastic peanut butter jar with lid
Water
Small stones
Rocks
Aquarium gravel
Sand
Plain index card

MATERIALS PER STUDENT

Student Lab Sheet 2.4
Pencil

PREPARATION

Have clean plastic peanut butter jars available (you can ask students to bring them in). Put rocks, stones, aquarium gravel, and sand in separate, easy-to-scoop-from containers. Duplicate Student Lab Sheet 2.4.

ANSWERS TO STUDENT LAB SHEET

1. The rocks are at the bottom. Because the rocks are the heaviest, they are unable to stay afloat as long as the lighter materials.
2. The sand is on the top. Because the sand is the lightest, it is able to be carried by the water for the longest period of time.

SUPER SCIENTIST ACTIVITIES

1. There is no written answer for this activity.
2. Students should use a simple balance for this activity. They will find that the material layers itself by weight.
3. Answers will vary. Students should take the measurement of each layer, divide this figure by the total measurement of all the layers, and then multiply the answer by 100. The result will be the particular layer's percent of the total.

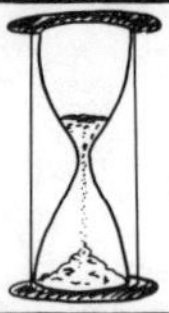

26

Running Hot, Then Cold

Students will discover that if limestone is heated (as if by the sun) and then cooled rapidly, it will start to break apart. This activity must be supervised by an adult!

MATERIALS PER LAB TEAM

Limestone (or other soft stone)
Tongs or spoon
Cold water
Hot plate
Clear jar (baby food or larger, depending on size of limestone)

MATERIALS PER STUDENT

Safety goggles
Student Lab Sheet 2.5
Pencil

PREPARATION

Duplicate Student Lab Sheet 2.5. Go over safety procedures for using a hot plate. Provide a control for the lab by placing one piece of unheated limestone in cold water. If necessary, discuss what a "control" is and why it is important for scientists to isolate variables. A control provides a point of reference. In this case, the control makes clear what breaks the limestone. Without the control, it would be impossible to know for certain whether it was the heat, the cold water, or the combination of the two that made the limestone break apart. If the cold water were the cause, the unheated limestone placed in the cold water would break. If heat alone were the cause, the limestone would break when it was heated in the pan. But if the limestone breaks only when it is heated and then cooled rapidly, we know that it was the change in temperature that caused the breaking. By providing a control, we were able to isolate each variable to form a conclusion.

ANSWERS TO STUDENT LAB SHEET

1. The hot plate represented the sun.
2. The limestone cracked and broke apart.
3. The limestone in the control jar did not break. The limestone that was heated and then cooled broke.
4. Heating the limestone caused it to expand, much like cement in a sidewalk expands on a hot day. The cold water caused the limestone to contract quickly. The rapid changing of size weakened the limestone and caused it to break.

SUPER SCIENTIST ACTIVITY

Answers will vary.

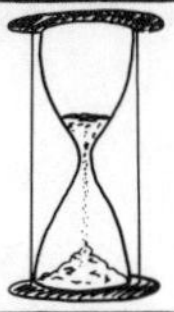

I'm Freezing

Freezing water plays a large part in soil formation. In this lab, students will see how water that freezes inside of limestone breaks the stone apart.

MATERIALS PER LAB TEAM

Limestone
Water
Plastic drinking glass
Plastic bag
Label
Permanent marker

MATERIALS PER STUDENT

Student Lab Sheet 2.6
Pencil

PREPARATION

Obtain access to a freezer in the school, and notify the teaching staff that you will be using the freezer for a science experiment. Duplicate Student Lab Sheet 2.6. Set up a control in front of the students (so they don't think you've done something magical). You can set up the control by following the procedures on the Student Lab Sheet *except* that you DO NOT put the control limestone in water.

ANSWERS TO STUDENT LAB SHEET

1. The limestone was soaked so that it could absorb water.
2. The limestone that was soaked in water and then placed in the freezer broke apart. The limestone that was placed in the freezer without first being soaked did not break.
3. The freezing water created pressure against the limestone and caused it to break. Water expands when it freezes, and it was this expansion that created the pressure on the limestone.

SUPER SCIENTIST ACTIVITIES

1. Answers will vary.
2. The size of the limestone should not affect the results of the lab experiment. It will affect the amount of water absorbed in the first Super Scientist Activity, however.

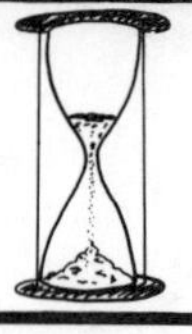

As Years Go By

In this lab, students will discover that soil is created very slowly. Because soil creation takes so long, in fact, soil conservation is a necessity.

MATERIALS PER STUDENT

Limestone or other soft stone, 2 pieces
Grocery bag
Student Lab Sheet 2.7
Pencil

PREPARATION

Obtain the limestone and grocery bags. Cut the grocery bags apart so that they become large sheets of brown paper. Duplicate Student Lab Sheet 2.7.

ANSWERS TO STUDENT LAB SHEET

1. Small particles of limestone fell on the bag.
2. It would take a *very long* time to fill a sandbox using this method.

SUPER SCIENTIST ACTIVITIES

1. Answers will vary.
2. Answers will vary, although students should realize that the harder the rock the longer it would take to produce particles on the bag.
3. Reports will vary. Students should, however, include facts about how wind and water break down rocks through erosion.

Student Lab Sheets

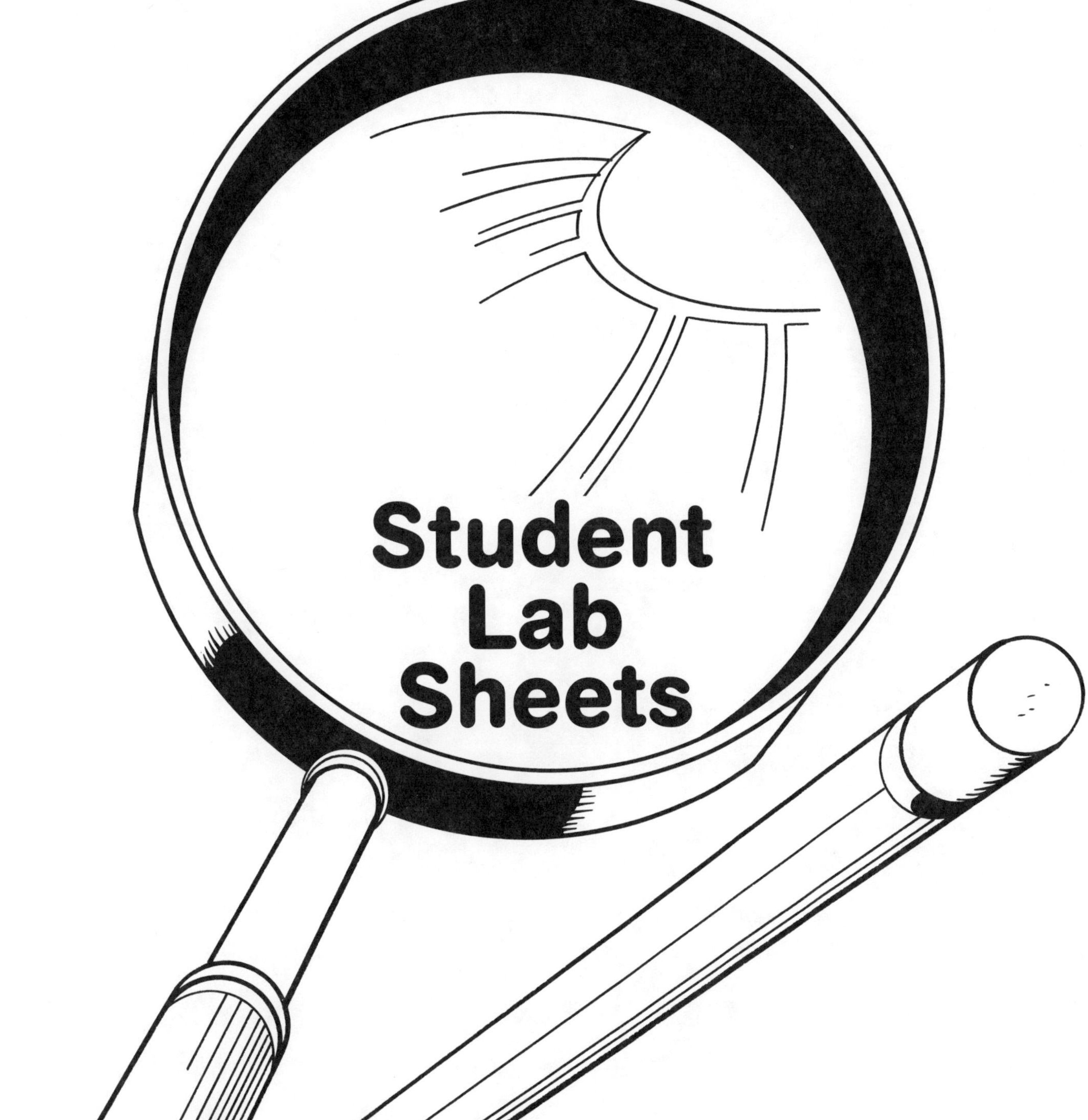

SOIL SCIENCE

Name ________________________ Date ________________________

Running Interference

Do animals affect the ground? In this lab, you will time the water absorption rate in an area used by animals and compare your finding with the rate for an area not used by animals.

MATERIALS

Two soup cans (ends removed)
Centimeter ruler
Water
Plastic drinking glass
Empty 35mm film container
Watch with second hand
Pencil

PROCEDURES

1. Choose an area that shows evidence of a lot of animal activity.
2. Push the soup can 3cm into the ground.
3. Fill the film container with water and empty it into the plastic drinking glass. Repeat this step 19 more times.
4. Empty the glass of water into the soup can.
5. Record how long it takes for the ground to absorb all the water.
6. Repeat steps 2-5 in an area that shows no evidence of animal activity.
7. Compare the rates of water absorption in the two areas.

RECORD YOUR OBSERVATIONS

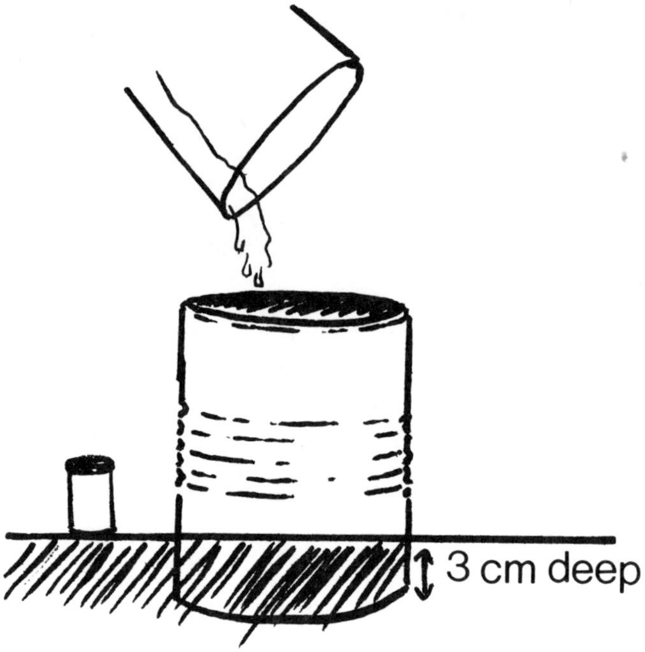

QUESTIONS TO ANSWER

1. How are the two areas you chose different?

___

___

___

2. Which area absorbed water more quickly?

___

___

___

SUPER SCIENTIST ACTIVITIES

1. Graph the amount of time required for all of the water to be absorbed in each location.
2. Repeat the experiment after a rainy day. Is there any difference in the water absorption rates?

Name ______________________________ Date ______________________ STUDENT LAB SHEET 2.2

Hold It!

Is all soil the same? In this lab, you will collect a soil sample from the schoolyard and find out how much water it contains. Then you will compare the amount of water in your sample with the amount of water in other students' samples.

MATERIALS

Spade
Empty 35mm film container
Baby food jar with lid
Label
Pencil

PROCEDURES

1. Decide where you will collect the sample of soil.
2. Use the spade to loosen the earth.
3. Fill the film container with soil.
4. Empty the soil from the film container into the baby food jar.
5. Tighten the lid on the jar.
6. Label the jar with your name and the place where you collected the soil.
7. Put the jar in a warm place and then *do not touch it!*

RECORD YOUR OBSERVATIONS

QUESTIONS TO ANSWER

1. What was on the sides of the jar?

2. Where did the water come from?

3. Which soil retained the most water?

4. How does a soil's ability to absorb water affect erosion?

SUPER SCIENTIST ACTIVITIES

1. Collect and measure all the water that formed inside the jar.
2. Repeat the experiment using soil from around the community.
3. Compare soil particle size to the soil's ability to retain water. What generalizations can you make?

Name ______________________ Date ______________________ STUDENT LAB SHEET 2.3

Drinking It All In

Do all types of soil absorb water at the same rate? How can you find out? In this lab, you will test soil in different locations to find out which one absorbs water most quickly.

MATERIALS

Soup can with both ends removed
Water
Watch with second hand
Empty 35mm film container
Centimeter ruler
Permanent marker
Plastic drinking glass
Pencil

PROCEDURES

1. Locate an area to test.
2. Push the can into the ground up to the 3cm mark.
3. Fill the film container with water and empty it into the plastic drinking glass. Repeat this step 19 more times.
4. Empty the glass of water into the can.
5. Time how long it takes for the soil to absorb all the water.

RECORD YOUR OBSERVATIONS

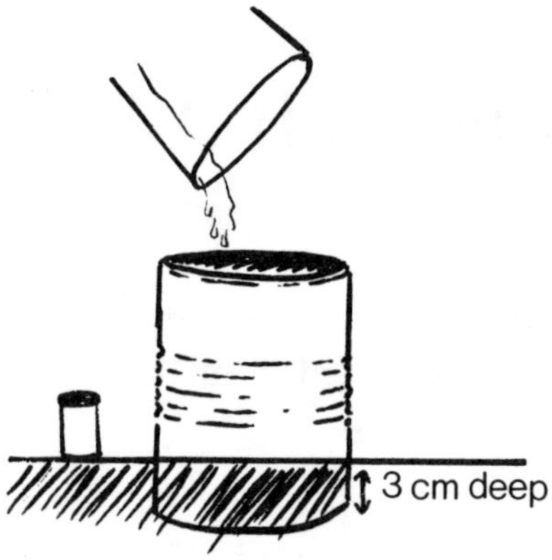

QUESTIONS TO ANSWER

1. Why did you use a can to pour the water into?

____

____

2. Why did everyone mark the cans at three centimeters?

____

____

____

3. How long did it take for the soil to absorb the water?

____

4. Did everyone get the same results? Why or why not?

____

____

____

5. Why is it better for soil to absorb water quickly?

____

____

____

SUPER SCIENTIST ACTIVITIES

1. Create a line graph that shows the different time each student's soil took to absorb the water.
2. Repeat the experiment after it has rained. Are the results the same?
3. Repeat the experiment at your home. Are the results the same?

Name ______________________________ Date ______________________ STUDENT LAB SHEET 2.4

Just Weight!

The Earth is made up of layers (kind of like a layer cake!). Is there any order to these layers? In this lab, you will observe soil particles and how they form layers.

MATERIALS

Plastic peanut butter jar with lid
Water
Small stones
Rocks
Aquarium gravel
Sand
Plain index card
Pencil

PROCEDURES

1. Fill the jar about two-thirds full of water.
2. Put in two handfuls of sand.
3. Do the same for the aquarium gravel, stones, and rocks.
4. Screw the lid on tightly and shake for two minutes.
5. Set the jar on a flat surface and let the contents settle (this may take awhile).
6. Hold up the index card vertically beside the jar, and mark the location of each layer on it.

RECORD YOUR OBSERVATIONS

QUESTIONS TO ANSWER

1. What was the bottom layer? Why?

___

___

___

2. What was the top layer? Why?

___

___

___

SUPER SCIENTIST ACTIVITIES

1. Examine evidence of soil layering in the schoolyard. Dig a shovel into the ground and tilt back the section of earth so that you can examine it.
2. Is there a relationship between a layer's weight and its position?
3. Calculate the percent each layer makes up of the total.

Name ______________________ Date ______________________ STUDENT LAB SHEET 2.5

Running Hot, Then Cold

Each day, the Earth is warmed by the sun. Each night, the Earth cools down. What effect does this heating and cooling have on the surface of the Earth? This activity, which must be done with an adult, will provide the answer.

MATERIALS

Limestone
Tongs or spoon
Cold water
Hot plate
Clear jar
Safety goggles
Pencil

PROCEDURES

1. Put a piece of limestone in a pan.
2. Put the pan on a hot plate (set to medium).
3. Allow the limestone to heat. *Watch carefully!*
4. Using tongs or a spoon, *carefully* remove the limestone from the pan.
5. Drop the piece of heated limestone into a jar of cold water.

RECORD YOUR OBSERVATIONS

QUESTIONS TO ANSWER

1. What, in nature, did the hot plate represent?

2. What did you observe happening in the jar?

3. How did the heated limestone differ from the piece used as a control?

4. Can you explain the results?

SUPER SCIENTIST ACTIVITY

Calculate the water temperature in the jar before and after adding the heated limestone. What is the difference in temperature?

Name ______________________________ Date ______________________

STUDENT LAB SHEET 2.6

I'm Freezing

What happens when water freezes in the surface of the Earth? In this simulation, you will find out without waiting for another Ice Age!

MATERIALS

Limestone
Water
Plastic drinking glass
Plastic bag
Label
Permanent marker
Pencil

PROCEDURES

1. Fill the glass half full of water.
2. Put a piece of limestone into the glass. Allow it to soak in the water for five minutes.
3. Remove the stone from the glass of water and put it in a plastic bag.
4. Label the bag with your name.
5. Put the bag in the freezer overnight.
6. The next day, take the bag out of the freezer and observe.

RECORD YOUR OBSERVATIONS

QUESTIONS TO ANSWER

1. Why did you soak the limestone?

2. What happened to the limestone that you soaked compared to the one used as a control?

3. How was the limestone affected by frozen water?

   Why?

SUPER SCIENTIST ACTIVITIES

1. Weigh the limestone before and after soaking. How much water did it absorb?
2. Repeat the experiment using limestone pieces of different sizes. Do you get the same results?

Name ______________________ Date ______________________

STUDENT LAB SHEET 2.7

As Years Go By

Think of the sand in a sandbox. How long would you guess it took to form that much sand? Then think about all the sand that erodes from the beach. How long would it take to replace all of it? In this lab, you will try to find the answers!

MATERIALS

Limestone, 2 pieces
Grocery bag
Pencil

PROCEDURES

1. Hold one piece of limestone in each hand.
2. Rub the pieces together over the brown paper.
3. Observe.

RECORD YOUR OBSERVATIONS

QUESTIONS TO ANSWER

1. What happened as you rubbed the pieces of limestone together?

2. How long would it take you to fill a sandbox by rubbing pieces of limestone?

SUPER SCIENTIST ACTIVITIES

1. Calculate how much soil you could make in ten minutes, an hour, a day, and a year.
2. How would the results of this experiment change if you used different types of rock?
3. Write a short report on how this process of soil formation takes place in nature.

LIFE SCIENCE

Don't Bug Me!

Children love races, and in this race the contestants have three left feet! They also have three right feet! Who will win? In this lab, students race insects that they have captured in search of a grand champion.

MATERIALS PER STUDENT

Race track (at least one per class)
Bug catcher (a jar will suffice)
Student Lab Sheet 3.1
Pencil

PREPARATION

Duplicate Student Lab Sheet 3.1. Draw a circular race track on a large piece of poster board. A track with a bull's-eye shape works best because it's hard to train an insect to go on a straight path! If necessary, review the characteristics that make an animal an insect. At this level, it is sufficient that students know that insects are invertebrates with three body parts and six legs. Now is also a good time to warn about insects that can sting or bite. Be sure to remind students that insects are living organisms and should be treated with respect. At the conclusion of the race, students should return all contestants back to their original environment–alive!

ANSWERS TO STUDENT LAB SHEET

1. Students will need to use an insect identification guide to answer this question. To provide additional practice in research skills, have students reference their source.
2. Insects, like children, can be very unpredictable. They seldom move in a straight line.
3. No, some insects fly, some crawl, some move fast while others are deliberate in their movements.

SUPER SCIENTIST ACTIVITIES

1. Dances will depend on the creativity of your students and how uninhibited they are!
2. Answers will vary depending on the insects chosen. Look for accurate labeling on the chart and for the presentation of correct information.

Critter Cuisine

What animals reside around your school? By setting out a variety of edibles, students can observe and determine which food is a "critter favorite." As an added attraction, students may even get the opportunity to observe their guests dining out.

MATERIALS PER CLASS

Variety of "critter food" (e.g., seeds of all kinds, raw vegetables and fruits, nuts, breads, dry cereal, crackers)

MATERIALS PER LAB TEAM

Empty 35mm film container
Styrofoam plate

MATERIALS PER STUDENT

Student Lab Sheet 3.2
Pencil

PREPARATION

Involve students in selecting the foods to set out. You can even ask students to bring in something that they feel would be appealing to an animal. Duplicate Student Lab Sheet 3.2.

ANSWERS TO STUDENT LAB SHEET

1. Answers will vary depending on the environment and the food provided.
2. Answers will vary depending on the environment and the food provided.
3. Answers will vary depending on the environment and the food provided.

SUPER SCIENTIST ACTIVITIES

1. Graphs will be specific to your class. Check that students have completed the graph accurately and labeled both axes correctly.
2. Graphs will be specific to your class. Check that students have completed the graph accurately and labeled both axes correctly.
3. Results will vary with the location of the food.

48

Are You Alive or Not?

This lab will sharpen students' observational skills as they classify objects into living and nonliving. This is a great follow-up activity to a unit on living and nonliving objects.

MATERIALS PER LAB TEAM

Hula hoop

MATERIALS PER STUDENT

Student Lab Sheet 3.3
Pencil

PREPARATION

Obtain hula hoops for students to use; check with the PE department or even ask the students if they have any. If you can't find hula hoops, substitute string tied into circles. Duplicate Student Lab Sheet 3.3.

ANSWERS TO STUDENT LAB SHEET

1. Answers will vary. Students should be able to justify their answers.
2. Answers will vary. Students should be able to justify their answers.
3. Answers will vary.

SUPER SCIENTIST ACTIVITIES

1. Food chains will vary. In general, a food chain includes a producer (any green plant), a primary consumer (animal that eats plants), a secondary consumer (animal that eats other animals), and a decomposer (such as fungus).
2. Graphs will be specific to your class. Check that students have completed the graph accurately and labeled both axes correctly.

Take A Hike!

To sharpen students' awareness of the outdoors, take a hike (a nature hike, that is)! In this hike, students will be looking for objects in nature that correspond to certain numbers, such as a branch with five leaves or an ant with six legs. By having specific objects to look for, students will less likely become distracted. But be sure to encourage creativity!

MATERIALS PER STUDENT

Student Lab Sheet 3.4
Pencil
Magnifying glass (optional)

PREPARATION

Discuss with students what a scavenger hunt is. Explain that the goal of this scavenger hunt is to find an object that represents each number from one to ten. If necessary, give examples. If students are too young to write down the names of what they find, have an older student assist (great for the older student's self-concept). Duplicate Student Lab Sheet 3.4.

ANSWERS TO STUDENT LAB SHEET

1. Answers will vary.
2. Answers will vary.

SUPER SCIENTIST ACTIVITIES

1. Answers will depend on your location.
2. Answers will depend on your location.

Halt! Who Goes There?

Animals are often scarce when humans are present (especially if you have planned an animal-observation field trip!). But even when you can't see them, animals often leave evidence of their existence. In this lab, students will become detectives as they locate and identify animal tracks.

MATERIALS PER LAB TEAM

Magnifying glass

MATERIALS PER STUDENT

Student Lab Sheet 3.5
Pencil

PREPARATION

This lab is more productive when the ground is soft—i.e., following a rain. Have a resource book on animal tracks available for students to examine. Duplicate Student Lab Sheet 3.5.

ANSWERS TO STUDENT LAB SHEET

1. Answers will vary.
2. Answers will vary.
3. Answers will vary. Some possible reasons would include animals looking for food, water, or shelter.
4. Besides footprints, students may find animal droppings, hair, feathers, twigs broken by passing animals, or half-eaten pieces of food.

SUPER SCIENTIST ACTIVITIES

1. There is no written answer. Show students how to pour a small amount of plaster of Paris into a paper cup (about an inch deep). Slowly add water while mixing. The plaster is ready to use when it is about the consistency of soft-serve ice cream. Pour the plaster of Paris into the track and allow it to dry. Then carefully remove it. The result is a fossil cast of an animal track.
2. Logs will vary.
3. Food chains will vary. In general, a food chain includes a producer (any green plant), a primary consumer (animal that eats plants), a secondary consumer (animal that eats other animals), and a decomposer (such as fungus).

Bag It!

Although we don't notice it, plants give off large quantities of water each day. Most of this water (given off in a process called transpiration) originally came from the soil by way of the plant's roots. In this lab, students will collect and measure the water given off by a branch.

MATERIALS PER LAB TEAM

Leafy branch
Plastic bag (one-gallon capacity or larger)
Heavy string
Measuring cup
Permanent marker

MATERIALS PER STUDENT

Student Lab Sheet 3.6
Pencil

PREPARATION

Duplicate Student Lab Sheet 3.6.

ANSWERS TO STUDENT LAB SHEET

1. The water came from the branch's leaves.
2. Answers will vary.

SUPER SCIENTIST ACTIVITIES

1. The branch with no leaves will not put as much water into the bag.
2. Answers will vary depending on the size and type of plant.

Lights, Camera, Action!

Photosynthesis takes place all around us without much fanfare. Yet without it, most life on Earth would quickly die. Photosynthesis requires light, but not all light will work. In this lab, students will discover that plants must have red light or natural sunlight if photosynthesis is to occur.

MATERIALS PER LAB TEAM

Plastic report covers in red, clear, green
Masking tape
Green plant

MATERIALS PER STUDENT

Student Lab Sheet 3.7
Pencil

PREPARATION

Cut the report covers in half across the width so that the fold makes up one side of each half. Duplicate Student Lab Sheet 3.7.

ANSWERS TO STUDENT LAB SHEET

1. Answers will vary, but the leaves in the red and clear report covers will be in the most natural condition.
2. Answers will vary, but the leaves in the red and clear report covers will be in the most natural condition.
3. Answers will vary, but the leaves in the red and clear report covers will be in the most natural condition.
4. Plants need red light or natural sunlight for photosynthesis to occur.

SUPER SCIENTIST ACTIVITIES

1. Reports will vary, but each should be in the student's own words.
2. Charts will vary. Make sure that all are properly labeled.

The Game of Life

Many creatures live in the soil. Most go unnoticed . . . until this lab! Students will scrutinize clumps of soil to determine what lives there.

MATERIALS PER LAB TEAM

Magnifying glass
Shovel

MATERIALS PER STUDENT

Student Lab Sheet 3.8
Pencil

PREPARATION

Get permission to "dig in the dirt" on school property. Remind students to return the soil to the same location from which they dug it out. Duplicate Student Lab Sheet 3.8.

ANSWERS TO STUDENT LAB SHEET

1. Answers will vary.
2. Answers will vary.
3. Answers will vary.
4. Answers will vary.

SUPER SCIENTIST ACTIVITIES

1. Maps will vary. Students should label all their "finds." Remind students to draw their maps to scale.
2. Graphs will vary depending on the specimens found. Make sure that students create bar graphs and that they label the axes.
3. Comparisons will vary.

Student Lab Sheets

LIFE SCIENCE

Name ______________________ Date ______________________

STUDENT LAB SHEET 3.1

Don't Bug Me!

It's a race! Who will win? You are the audience *and* the cheering section as you race insects in search of a grand champion.

MATERIALS

Race track
Bug catcher (a jar with holes in the lid is fine)
Pencil

PROCEDURES

1. Search for an insect that you think is fast.
2. *Carefully* catch the insect in a jar. Fasten the lid to keep the insect inside, but make sure the holes in the lid allow plenty of air for the insect to breathe.
3. Allow your insect to get out of the jar in the center of the race track with three other contestants.
4. See which insect moves the fastest to the outside of the track.
5. If your insect is a winner, race it against other winners until one insect becomes the grand champion for the class.
6. Return your contestant unharmed back to where you found it.

RECORD YOUR OBSERVATIONS

QUESTIONS TO ANSWER

1. What kind of insect did you choose?

2. Did the insects move in a straight line?

3. Do all insects move in the same way?

SUPER SCIENTIST ACTIVITIES

1. Create an "Insect Dance." Use your whole body to imitate how different insects move.
2. Make a chart identifying the insects in the races. On the chart, indicate which insects came in first, second, and third place.

Critter Cuisine

What animals live around your school? What is their favorite treat for lunch? This lab will help you to find out!

MATERIALS

"Critter" food
Empty 35mm film container
Styrofoam plate
Pencil

PROCEDURES

1. Decide what critter food you will provide.
2. Fill a 35mm film container with the food. Then empty the contents of the film container onto a plate.
3. Put the plate outside where critters can get to the food.
4. Observe the critters that come to eat off the plate.
5. Measure the amount of food remaining each day. Add more if necessary, but don't forget to measure the food you add!

RECORD YOUR OBSERVATIONS

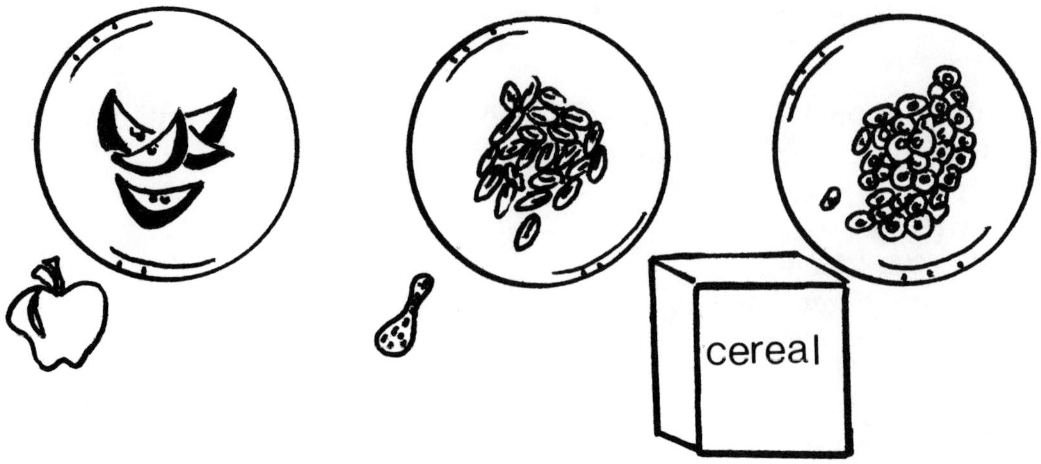

QUESTIONS TO ANSWER

1. What animals did you observe?

____

____

2. Which food was the critters' favorite?

____

____

3. How much of your food did the animals eat each day?

____

____

SUPER SCIENTIST ACTIVITIES

1. Graph the total amount of food consumed each day.
2. Graph the amount of each kind of food consumed on one day.
3. Move the location of the food. Do the results stay the same?

Name ______________________________ Date ______________________________

STUDENT LAB SHEET 3.3

Are You Alive or Not?

How well can you classify objects? Try your skill with this lab as you classify objects into living and nonliving.

MATERIALS

Hula hoop (or a string tied in a circle)
Pencil

PROCEDURES

1. Lay the plastic or string circle on the ground.
2. Make a list of everything you can find inside the circle that is alive or was once alive.
3. Make a list of everything you can find inside the circle that was never alive.

RECORD YOUR OBSERVATIONS

QUESTIONS TO ANSWER

1. What did you find that is/was alive?

____

____

2. What did you find that was never alive?

____

____

3. Which list is longer?

____

SUPER SCIENTIST ACTIVITIES

1. Create a food chain from the things you found in the circle.
2. Make a graph of the living and nonliving items you found.

Name ______________________ Date ______________________

STUDENT LAB SHEET 3.4

Take A Hike!

In this lab, you will take a hike outside, looking for objects in nature that correspond to certain numbers. For example, you might find a branch with five leaves or an ant with six legs. Your goal is to find an object that represents each number from one to ten.

MATERIALS

Pencil
Magnifying glass (optional)

PROCEDURES

While on your nature hike, record something you see that corresponds to each number:

1 ______________________

2 ______________________

3 ______________________

4 ______________________

5 ______________________

6 ______________________

7 ______________________

8 ______________________

9 ______________________

10 ______________________

QUESTIONS TO ANSWER

1. What number was the easiest to fill in?

____

2. What number was the hardest?

____

SUPER SCIENTIST ACTIVITIES

1. Go on another hike. This time make it an alphabet hike. Can you find an object in nature that corresponds to each letter of the alphabet?
2. Go on a color hike. Can you find something in nature that corresponds to each color in an eight-count box of crayons?

Name ______________________ Date ______________________ STUDENT LAB SHEET 3.5

Halt! Who Goes There?

Animals often hide when people are around, but they leave evidence of their existence in footprints. Become a detective and identify animal tracks on the school property!

MATERIALS

Magnifying glass
Pencil

PROCEDURES

1. *Carefully* search the area for animal tracks.
2. When you find an animal footprint, draw it on your paper.
3. Identify the animal that left the track.

RECORD YOUR OBSERVATIONS

QUESTIONS TO ANSWER

1. What animals (besides humans) use the school property?

2. Which class of animals appears most frequently?

3. Why are the animals on the school property?

4. What other evidence of animal life can you find?

SUPER SCIENTIST ACTIVITIES

1. Make a plaster of Paris cast of any animal track you find. Start a collection for the class to examine.
2. Keep a daily log of the tracks you find.
3. Design a food chain of the animals that live on school property.

Name ______________________ Date ______________________ STUDENT LAB SHEET 3.6

Bag It!

Take a close look at a plant. See anything happening? Although you might not see it, the plant is giving off water. The process of a plant giving off water is called transpiration. In this lab, you will collect and measure the water given off by a branch.

MATERIALS

Leafy branch
Plastic bag (one-gallon capacity or larger)
Heavy string
Measuring cup
Permanent marker
Pencil

PROCEDURES

1. Use the marker to write your name on the bag.
2. Carefully put the bag around a leafy branch.
3. Tie the open end of the bag with string so that the branch is completely sealed in the bag.
4. Leave the branch in the bag overnight (or longer).
5. *Carefully* remove the bag from the branch.
6. Pour all the water that has collected in the bag into the measuring cup.
7. Compare your results with other teams.

RECORD YOUR OBSERVATIONS

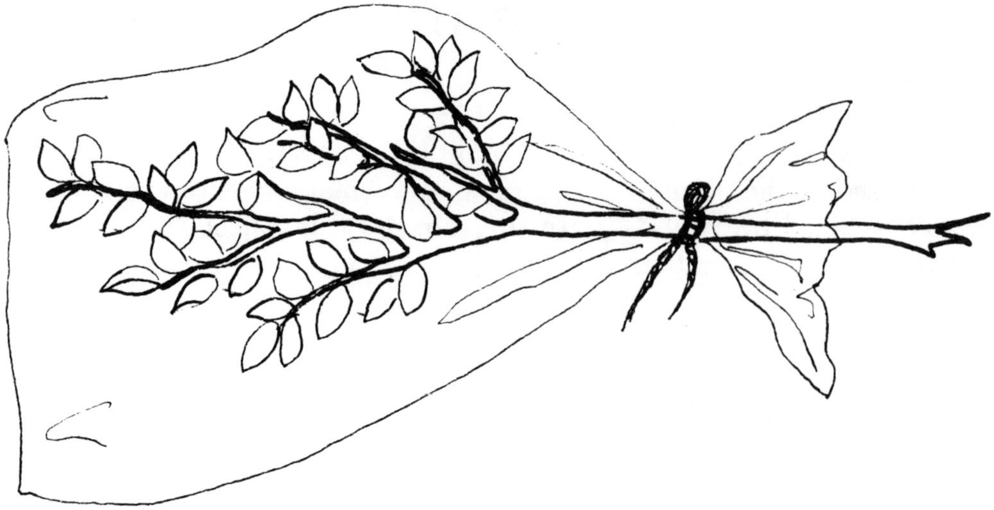

QUESTIONS TO ANSWER

1. Where did the water in the bag come from?

2. What tree gave off the most water?

SUPER SCIENTIST ACTIVITIES

1. Repeat the experiment, but this time use a branch that has no leaves. Compare the results.
2. Set up an experiment to see if the size of the branch affects the amount of water that collects in the bag.

Name ______________________ Date ______________________

STUDENT
LAB
SHEET 3.7

Lights, Camera, Action!

Photosynthesis is taking place all around us, but we scarcely know it occurs. Without it, however, most life on Earth would quickly die. Photosynthesis requires light, but only light of a certain color will work. In this lab, you will be experimenting with plants to find out what color the light must be.

MATERIALS

Plastic report covers in red, clear, green
Leaves from a living green plant
Masking tape
Pencil

PROCEDURES

1. Turn one plastic cover so that the fold is on the left.
2. Tape the cover's top and bottom edges closed.
3. Slip a living leaf (still attached to a small branch) into the cover.
4. Tape the cover's remaining edge closed.
5. Repeat steps 1-4 for the two other covers.
6. Keep the leaves in the covers for one week. Then remove and compare them.

RECORD YOUR OBSERVATIONS

QUESTIONS TO ANSWER

1. How do the leaves compare in color?

____

____

____

2. How do the leaves compare in size and shape?

____

____

____

3. How do the leaves compare in stiffness?

____

____

____

4. What color light do plants need for photosynthesis?

____

____

SUPER SCIENTIST ACTIVITIES

1. Repeat the experiment using report covers in different colors of plastic. Write up your results.
2. Make a chart of your observations.

Name ______________________ Date ______________________

STUDENT LAB SHEET 3.8

The Game of Life

Many creatures live in the soil. Most go unnoticed . . . until today! In this lab, you will study a clump of soil to try to discover what lives there.

MATERIALS

Magnifying glass
Shovel
Pencil

PROCEDURES

1. Use the shovel to tilt upward a triangular section of soil about 20cm wide by 40cm deep.
2. Look closely at the soil for signs of life.
3. Categorize and count each specimen you find.
4. *Replace the soil so that it is as undisturbed as possible!*

RECORD YOUR OBSERVATIONS

QUESTIONS TO ANSWER

1. What type of life was at the top of the soil?

2. What type of life was at the bottom of the soil?

3. Where did you find most of the life?

4. What type of life was the most abundant?

SUPER SCIENTIST ACTIVITIES

1. Draw a "map" of your section of soil. Mark the location of any life you found.
2. Use a bar graph to show the number of each specimen you found.
3. Examine a section of soil near a stream or in the woods and compare your findings.

ENVIRONMENTAL SCIENCE

Litter By Litter

How often do students drop pieces of paper on the ground without a second thought? After this lab, the school litter problem may be reduced. Students will test the biodegradability of litter they find outdoors.

MATERIALS PER LAB TEAM

Junior-size baby food jar
Piece of paper litter
Tape

MATERIALS PER STUDENT

Student Lab Sheet 4.1
Pencil

PREPARATION

Collect junior-size baby food jars. Wash and remove labels. Duplicate Student Lab Sheet 4.1. Have students do this lab together so that they can make comparisons.

ANSWERS TO STUDENT LAB SHEET

1. Answers will vary.
2. Answers will vary.
3. If the litter in the jar begins to break down into smaller pieces, it is biodegradable.

SUPER SCIENTIST ACTIVITIES

1. Answers will vary depending on the litter selected. Plastic litter will degrade at a much slower rate, if at all.
2. Your local government should be able to provide the name of the sanitation company that services your school. Contact the company directly.

Is Mother Nature A Litter Bug?

We all know that humans are litter bugs, but what about Mother Nature? Students will find out in this lab!

MATERIALS PER CLASS

White bed sheet
Rocks, at least 4
Magnifying glasses

MATERIALS PER STUDENT

Student Lab Sheet 4.2
Pencil

PREPARATION

Obtain a white sheet; you might check with your local hospital for discards. A pale pastel sheet will do if a white one is unavailable. Duplicate Student Lab Sheet 4.2.

ANSWERS TO STUDENT LAB SHEET

1. Answers will vary depending on your location.
2. Answers will vary.
3. In general, the items on the sheet were carried there by the air or by an animal.

SUPER SCIENTIST ACTIVITIES

1. Answers will vary.
2. Answers will vary.

Ah, A Breath of Fresh Air!

Take a deep breath. What did your lungs just take in (besides air, of course)? In this lab, students will trap tiny particles from the air both inside and outside the classroom and then compare their findings.

MATERIALS PER LAB TEAM

Index cards (3x5-inch), 2
Petroleum jelly
String
Ruler
Permanent marker, narrow
Magnifying glass

MATERIALS PER STUDENT

Student Lab Sheet 4.3
Pencil

PREPARATION

Show students how use the ruler and permanent marker to turn the index cards into grids made up of one-inch squares. When completed, each card should have 15 squares (an example appears on the Student Lab Sheet). Have students put their names on the opposite sides of the cards. Duplicate Student Lab Sheet 4.3.

ANSWERS TO STUDENT LAB SHEET

1. The card hung outdoors should have more particles trapped on it, but there will always be exceptions to this general rule!
2. Answers will vary depending on the location of the card.

SUPER SCIENTIST ACTIVITIES

1. Answers will vary.
2. Answers will vary.

Do You Hear What I Hear?

Stop, look, and listen. What do you hear? As students sit outside, they will try to identify the sounds they hear.

MATERIALS PER STUDENT

Student Lab Sheet 4.4
Pencil

PREPARATION

Remind students that they will need to sit quietly if they hope to hear any sounds. To develop students' listening skills, bring in records or tapes (commercial or homemade) of various sounds for students to identify. Duplicate Student Lab Sheet 4.4.

ANSWERS TO STUDENT LAB SHEET

1. Answers will vary according to the location.
2. Answers will vary.

SUPER SCIENTIST ACTIVITIES

1. Answers will vary. If possible, students should listen first thing in the day and then go back out late in the afternoon.
2. Play the tape!

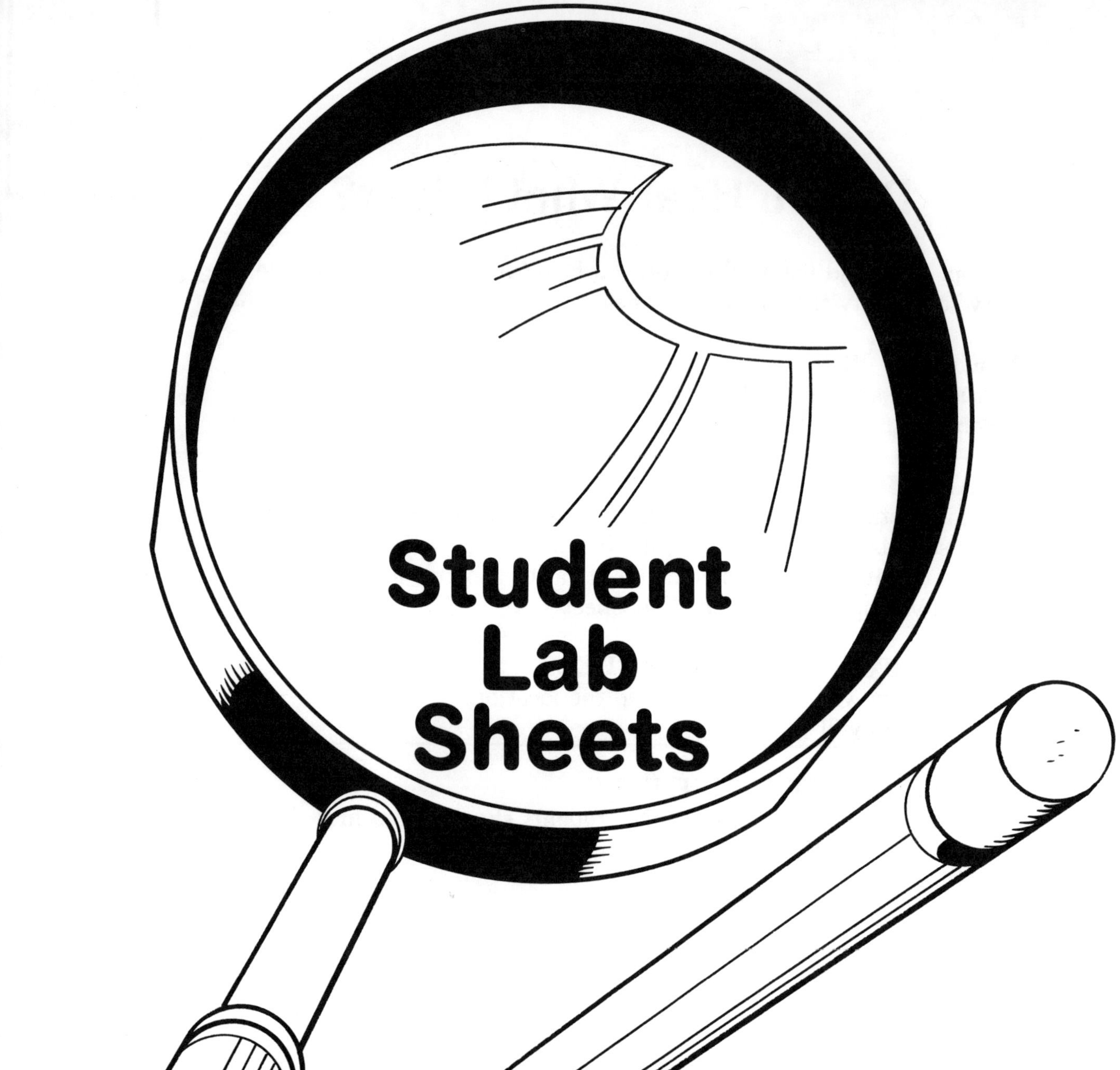

Student Lab Sheets

ENVIRONMENTAL SCIENCE

Name ______________________________ Date ______________________ STUDENT LAB SHEET 4.1

Litter By Litter

Do you ever drop paper on the schoolyard without thinking about it? What happens to that paper? In this lab, you will test the biodegradability of litter.

MATERIALS

Junior-size baby food jar
Piece of paper litter
Tape
Pencil

PROCEDURES

1. Collect paper litter from the schoolyard. Trim all of it to the same size for testing.
2. Attach a small piece of the paper being tested to the outside of the baby food jar for identification.
3. Fill the jar half full of water.
4. Put the litter inside the jar and fasten the lid on.
5. Shake the jar 30 times.
6. Compare the paper inside the jar with the piece attached to the outside.
7. Compare the paper in your jar with others in the class.
8. Leave the jar undisturbed for one week.
9. Repeat steps 5 through 8.

RECORD YOUR OBSERVATIONS

QUESTIONS TO ANSWER

1. What kind of paper changed the most?

   What kind of paper changed the least?

2. How did the papers change?

3. Is the litter on the school ground biodegradable?

SUPER SCIENTIST ACTIVITIES

1. Repeat this experiment using litter other than paper. What do you find?
2. Find out how your community treats solid wastes.

Name ______________________________ Date ______________________________

Is Mother Nature A Litter Bug?

We all know that humans are litter bugs, but what about Mother Nature? Is she a litter bug? Do this lab to find out!

MATERIALS

White bed sheet
Rocks, at least 4
Magnifying glass
Pencil

PROCEDURES

1. Spread open the sheet on an open area outside.
2. Put a weight (such as a rock) on each corner of the sheet.
3. Wait 24 hours and then examine the sheet.

RECORD YOUR OBSERVATIONS

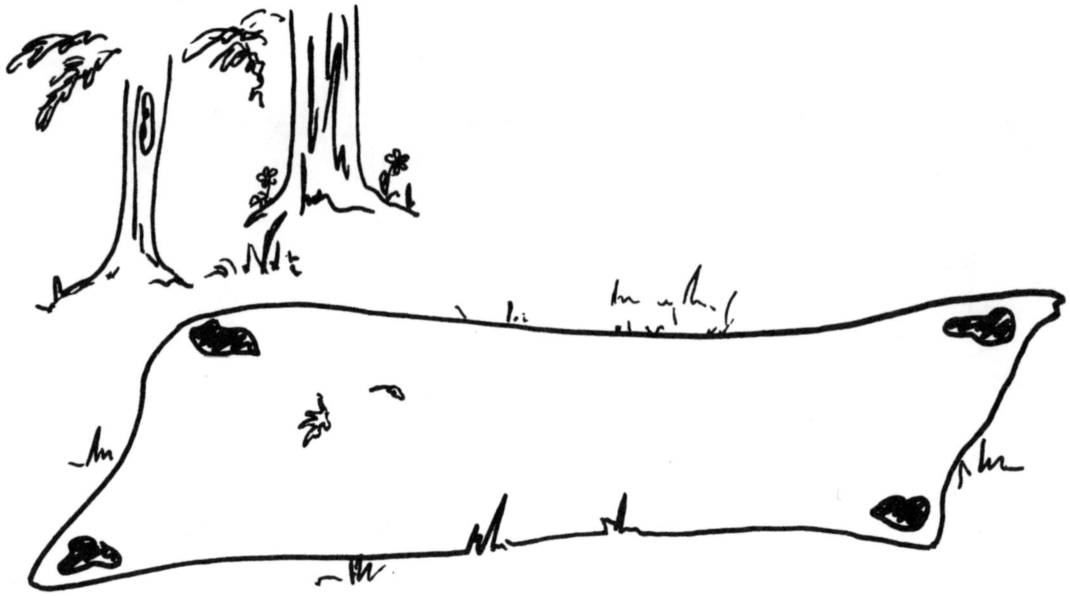

QUESTIONS TO ANSWER

1. What did you find on the sheet?

2. How many different things could you identify on the sheet?

3. How did the items on the sheet get there?

SUPER SCIENTIST ACTIVITIES

1. Spread out the sheet in a different location. Repeat the experiment and compare the results.
2. Repeat this lab in a month. Do you get the same results?

Name ______________________________ Date ______________________________

Ah, A Breath of Fresh Air!

Take a deep breath. What did you just take into your lungs—besides air, of course? You will know the answer after testing the air around your school in this lab!

MATERIALS

Index cards (3x5-inch), 2
Petroleum jelly
String
Ruler
Permanent marker, narrow
Magnifying glass
Pencil

PROCEDURES

1. Put a piece of string through each card, and then tie the string so that it makes a circle.
2. Spread petroleum jelly thinly on the squares side of each card.
3. Hang one card outside (in an out-of-the-way place) and one inside the classroom. Leave them alone for four days.
4. Choose one square *on each card* and count the number of particles (use a magnifying glass to help you see). Then do the same for nine more squares.
5. Add the total for the ten squares of each card and divide by ten. The result is the average number of particles per square on your outside card and your inside card.

RECORD YOUR OBSERVATIONS

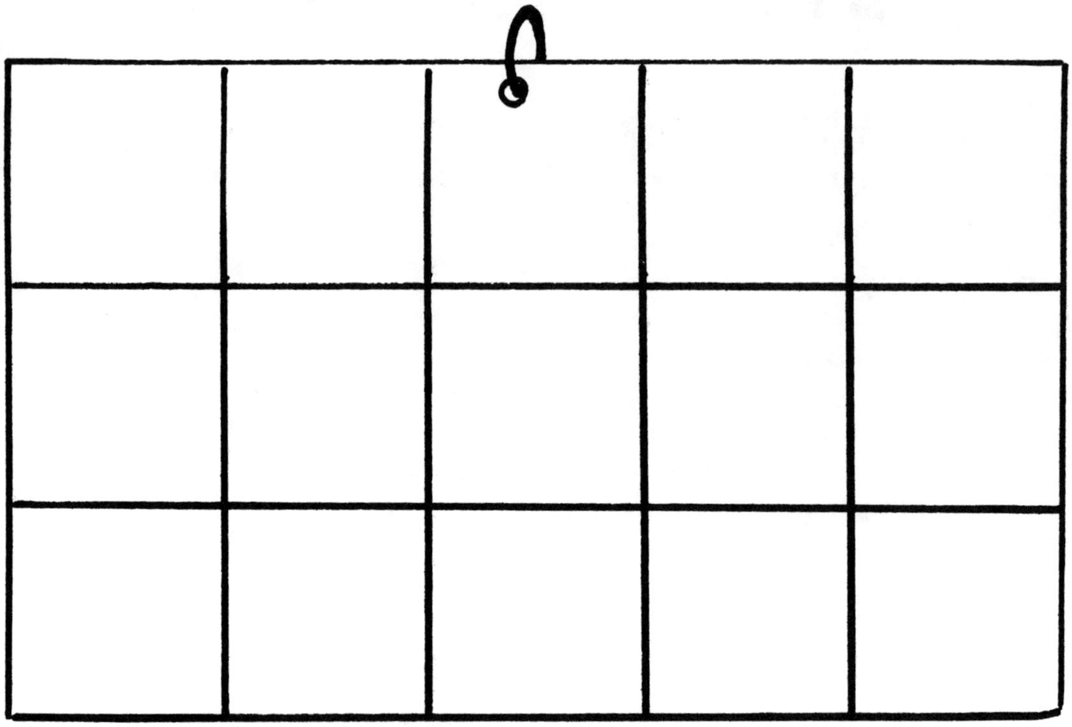

QUESTIONS TO ANSWER

1. How did the two cards compare in terms of the average number of particles per square?

2. What are the particles?

SUPER SCIENTIST ACTIVITIES

1. Repeat the experiment at home and compare the results.
2. Hang similar index cards around the community. What do you find?

Name ______________________________ Date ______________________

Do You Hear What I Hear?

Stop, look, and listen! What do you hear? In this lab, you will try to identify the sounds you hear in the great outdoors.

MATERIALS

Pencil

PROCEDURES

1. Find a spot outside where you can sit quietly and listen.
2. Listen carefully for five minutes.
3. Identify what makes each sound.
4. Make a list of the sounds you hear.

RECORD YOUR OBSERVATIONS

QUESTIONS TO ANSWER

1. Were most of the sounds you heard made by plants or by animals?

___

___

2. Could you identify the sounds you heard?

___

___

SUPER SCIENTIST ACTIVITIES

1. Repeat this activity at different times throughout the day. Compare your results.
2. Take a tape recorder outside and record sounds.